girls' NIGHT IN

FABULOUS IDEAS FOR EVENINGS WITH FRIENDS

girls' NIGHT IN

FABULOUS IDEAS FOR EVENINGS WITH FRIENDS

RYLAND
PETERS
& SMALL

LONDON NEW YORK

laura maffeo

photography by claire richardson

DESIGNER Pamela Daniels
EDITOR Miriam Hyslop
LOCATION RESEARCH Tracy Ogino
PRODUCTION MANAGER Patricia Harrington
ART DIRECTOR Anne-Marie Bulat
EDITORIAL DIRECTOR Julia Charles
PUBLISHING DIRECTOR Alison Starling

STYLIST Sally Conran
HAIR & MAKE-UP ARTIST Marie Anne Coulter

First published in the United States in 2006
by Ryland Peters & Small, Inc.
519 Broadway
5th Floor
New York NY 10012
10 9 8 7 6 5 4 3 2 1

Text, design, and photography
© Ryland Peters & Small 2006

ISBN-10: 1 84597 142 6
ISBN-13: 978 1 84597 142 7

Cataloging-in-Publication Data is available on
request from the Library of Congress.

Printed in China

contents

introduction

Gathering together is a long-standing tradition among women. It begins as teenagers, when girls and boys segregate at parties, girls on one side of the room and boys on the other. As young women enter the world of adulthood they make dates to hit the town for drinks and dining, parties, and dancing with friends.

When women settle down or get married, and make a home of their own, lives change. Love for their girlfriends strengthens and the need to connect with other women remains a priority. The only difference is that the ever popular girls' night out often becomes the girls' night in.

Single or married, youthful or sophisticated, women want ways in which to enjoy each other's company. It's simple. All you need is an evening, a theme, and a great group of girlfriends and you're on your way.

poker night

betting & bluffing

It used to be that only men would get together for a night of poker. It was cherished time away from the girls when they could just be boys. Well, why should the boys have all the fun? Just because we don't want to sit around drinking beer and chomping on cigars (well, maybe we do, but that's not the point) doesn't mean we girls can't enjoy a night of betting, bluffing, and going for the royal flush. Poker is great fun and an excellent way to see how well your friends can "bluff." Next time one of your girlfriends tells you she didn't borrow your favorite green sweater, you'll know if she's telling the truth...

CLEAR YOUR CHIPS OFF THE TABLE ...

... and opt for some great poker snacks that will be easy to grab and won't "mark" your cards. Why serve the average chips and dips when you can put a modern spin on old-fashioned nibbles? Choose a classic cocktail like a Cosmopolitan and pair it with some spicy Roasted Nuts (see recipes page 56). Instead of pretzels, try some easy homemade Cheese Straws. You don't have to spend a lot of time and money to put together a simple buffet that puts a fresh and feminine twist on the standard fare.

All you need is a deck of cards, some snacks, and your best poker face.

casino capers

Transforming a space into a casino can be done with little effort and cost. First, you'll need to cover a table with felt. This not only acts as a tablecloth, protecting the table from spills and scuffs, but also prevents cards from flying off the table as they are delt. Most casinos use green felt, but your home isn't most casinos. Get a couple of yards of pink felt for a femme-fabulous look.

Set up the snacks on a buffet close by so your guests can easily grab a bite in between hands. Decorate the buffet with a playing cards theme. Anything with hearts, diamonds, clubs, or spades is great. Dress up the scene by serving the snacks on your best silver or china. Place small vases of fragrant flowers around the room. Who says a card game can't have style?

TIPS

- *Use coupons instead of cash. Why spend hard-earned money when $1.00 off groceries works great, too? Before you start the game, "buy" your chips with $20 worth of coupons rather than cash. The winner takes all!*

- *Don't feel like dealing the cards? Hire someone's husband or boyfriend for the job. Get him a green visor and he's ready to deal.*

- *Bet with beauty. Instead of chips, bring all of your cosmetic samples and travel-sized products.*

- *Chips for chores! Instead of putting a monetary amount on your chips, barter for helpful tasks around the house. Winner gets the girls to help paint the bedroom? Be creative and willing to do the jobs. This is guaranteed to motivate your opponents to bet big!*

let the games begin!

One of the most popular poker games on the planet right now is Texas Hold 'Em. It's really easy to learn and fun to play with any number of people.

To start off, each player "antes" (places the opening bet before the cards are dealt) and is dealt two cards. You can then "check" (decide not to bet but stay in the hand), bet, or fold (forfeit the hand). Once someone else bets, you have to "call" (bet the same amount) or fold. After this, the dealer lays out three cards face up on the table. This is called the "flop." Each player then decides if they can make one of the hands listed opposite, by combining the two cards in their hand with the three in the flop. In turn, each player checks, bets, or folds. After this, the dealer adds another card face up to the flop. This is called the "turn." Again each player may check, bet, or fold. The last card turned up on the table is called the "river." Once all players have bet or folded, they reveal their cards to show who has the best hand.

Here's how each hand ranks, from lowest hand to highest:

A Pair

Two Pairs

Three of a Kind

A Straight Five numbers in order

A Flush Five cards of the same suit in no order

A Full House Three of a kind and a pair

Four of a Kind

A Straight Flush Five of a kind in numerical order

A Royal Flush Same as a Straight Flush but with an ace high

bedazzle it

glittering girls

Every girl wants to have the latest and greatest fashion accessories. Who doesn't love it when someone stops you to ask "where did you get that?" Think of the satisfaction you and your girlfriends will have when you can respond with "I made it myself!" By hosting a Bedazzle It night, you can combine a fun night in with the girls with making this season's fashion must-haves. It's relatively simple and quick to string together sparkly bead necklaces or to use a glue gun to create pretty hair clips.

Serve a glittering cocktail and some divine finger foods and you'll have a night of pure glamour! With some careful planning and a splash of creativity, you and your friends will soon be breathing new life into your wardrobes with unique, ready-to-wear accessories.

DAZZLING SNACKS

Food for a Bedazzle It night should be easy to snack on, so
you don't have to divert your attention away from your
fabulous projects. Set out Shrimp with Chilli Mojo for dipping
(see recipes page 57). Refreshing Spring Rolls are a great
treat to feed your guests as well. And what could be more
glamorous than a crisp Gibson Martini served in a chilled
martini glass (see recipes page 57)? As an alternative to
martinis, stir up a jug of fruit juices mixed with sparkling
water, and add fresh fruit garnishes in jewel colors.

ready, set, glam!

A Bedazzle It night takes a bit of planning and preparation to pull off, but it can be a glittering evening if you think ahead. First, you've got to decide what types of projects you'd like to do.

Are you and your friends more drawn to threaded jewelry like necklaces and bracelets? Would you rather simplify the night by sticking to things that only require glue, such as barrettes, ponytail holders, and headbands?

Once you've decided, it's time to make up a list of supplies. If you are trying to keep the costs down, ask your friends to chip in to the "glamour fund" a few weeks ahead of the day so you can go out and pick up all of the supplies at once. Bead shops are a great resource for everything you will need. It is also more economical if you buy in larger quantities. This way, you can all share the supplies and there aren't as many unnecessary left-overs. Usually you end up with more than you need of things like jewelry findings and wire.

After you've gathered together all that you need for your projects, throw a basic tablecloth over your table surface to protect it from glue and scuffs. Place beads and other small items in bowls and baskets in the center of the table. This makes them cute to display and easy to get to. If you only have a smaller space to work in, shoe-box tops make great trays for beading projects. The girls can grab beads and tools and work on their laps.

TIPS

- *If you're sending out invitations, add a playful spin by attaching a candy necklace to it. Adorable and tasty!*

- *Ask your friends to raid their jewelry boxes. Perhaps that old beaded necklace might be better used for parts to create a fresh look? Have everyone donate to a communal jewelry collection you can all share in.*

- *Make sure to ask your guests to bring along any spare pairs of scissors, pliers, and glue guns. That way, there are plenty to go around and everyone can work at once.*

- *Have small hand mirrors around so your friends can admire their creations and check lengths and styles.*

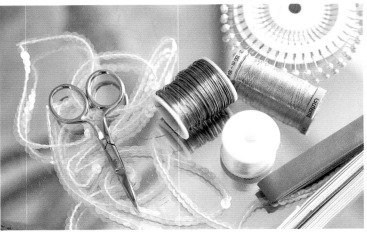

sparkling style

The following are some super easy and oh-so-stylish projects you and your girlfriends can pull together in a flash. You'll need to have a few tools handy before you get going. Make sure you've got a glue gun and glue sticks, scissors, and pliers. Do a little fashion homework by scouring the pages of your favorite fashion magazines to transform your projects into this season's key accessories. Choose colors and bead styles to reflect the latest looks.

EASY BEADED LARIAT

You should have enough flexible jewelry wire for your desired-length necklace. Starting on one end, string on one crimp bead. Follow it with a bead that will be at least ½ inch in diameter. This will be the end of the lariat that you string through the loop on the other end to secure it. Once you've done this, follow that bead with a tiny one just larger than the hole of the big bead. Take the end of the wire and string it around the tiny bead and back up through the large bead and crimp bead. The tiny bead is now holding the big bead onto the wire. Crimp the crimp bead with small pliers. This secures this end. Trim excess wire. Now you can bead whatever styles and colors you wish to the length you wish. Once you have reached the end, add one crimp bead and then string enough tiny beads so that you can create a loop that will just fit

around your big bead at the other end. String the end of the wire back through the crimp bead, pull wire tightly, and crimp with pliers.

OTHER IDEAS

Other simple projects can be created using just a glue gun. Find the latest-colored silk flowers and glue onto metal barrette bases for a dramatic hair accessory. Glue a small cluster of flowers onto a ponytail holder for a feminine twist on an everyday item. Using simple leather or suede string, hang a large bead or shell to make a fresh summer pendant.

Find the latest colored silk flowers and glue onto metal barrette bases for a dramatic hair accessory.

spa night

take me away

Self-indulgence is a favorite pastime for most women. There is not a girl out there who would turn down a good facial massage or killer pedicure. With modern life as hectic as it is, there never seems to be enough time in the day to get everything done and still allow yourself a relaxing ''me'' moment to recharge your batteries.

So why not treat yourself and your girlfriends to a home spa night? Enjoy the luxury of unwinding with a good neck rub, trying a great nail color, and taking time out in the company of your favorite women. Serve a refreshing drink and some healthful snacks and your friends will be in spa heaven. Whip up a few easy and inexpensive home spa treatments and witness the welcome return of a glow to your cheeks and pep in your step.

SPA SNACKING

Putting together a home spa menu is a snap. We all know that simple and fresh ingredients are the key to spa snacking. The trick is to mix things up so it doesn't feel like you are feeding your guests the same old fruit and vegetables. Try blending together a variety of frozen fruit and fruit juice to create frosty smoothies. Serve delicious sushi with your choice of filling or Hummus and Flatbeans (see recipes page 58) along with dishes of fresh fruit and nuts. Cut up a lemon, a lime, and a cucumber, and add to a large pitcher of iced water. During spa treatments, serve the girls a glass garnished with a sprig of fresh mint for an instant spa refresher. Once you've all been pampered and polished, wrap up in warm robes, lie back, and unwind with tall glasses of Mojitos (see recipes page 59). Remember that the goal here is to relax and enjoy.

fresh & fabulous

Why not hire professional beauty specialists? You should decide on a few different treatments and book them a few weeks beforehand. If you want to focus on beauty, hire a manicurist and makeup artist. If you are leaning towards relaxation and indulgence, make it a masseuse. If budget is an issue, scale down the professional treatments and prepare a "do-it-yourself" spa. Ask the girls to bring their favorite nail polishes to swap colors. Everyone has a mask or scrub at home. Bring them along to share. Also, tell the girls to bring their own robes and flip-flops for comfort. Plan well and you can relax and enjoy the night along with your girlfriends.

TIPS

- *If cost is an issue, you can "hire" different friends to be specialists. If you divide up the responsibilities, it lightens the burden both financially and time-wise. You can pick different departments for people to be in charge of. One person can bring cotton and manicure materials. Another friend can get the flip-flops from the drugstore. Someone else can supply the ingredients for a mask. If the hostess supplies the home and refreshments, it makes it easier to pull off fresh and fun spa "treatments" with the girls.*

- *A home spa night can also be a home spa day. Set up the treatment areas outside in the yard on a nice day and enjoy the weather while painting your toes. Who needs a tanning salon when you can get a nice glow from the sun? Remember always to wear your sunscreen!*

- *Turn a regular washcloth into a sumptuous spa experience by infusing it with chilled rose water. Simply boil some water with rose petals thrown in and then chill it. When you're ready, soak the cloths with the rose water and then roll up. Serve to your guests on small plates to cool and hydrate faces. If roses aren't your favorite, try fresh rosemary and mint for an herbal infusion.*

oasis of calm

It's easy to turn your home in to a Zen spa environment with cool, clean decor and lighting. Cover the furniture with sheets to keep everything clean and create a fresh spa look. Throw pillows around on the floor throughout the room to add a few more comfy seating areas. Also, have plenty of fresh towels standing by in baskets around the room. Use clear glassware and white flowers to keep the clean simplicity of a spa environment. Decorating with bowls of citrus fruit and stones also lends a more sleek and minimal style. It's a sophisticated look that is quite easy to put together.

Burn essential oil candles with aromas like cucumber or grapefruit. These scents help to ease tension and invigorate the senses. Avoid anything too heavily perfumed, as this can be a bit overwhelming along with the beauty products.

TREATMENTS

Home spa treatments are easy to mix up with ingredients found around the house and at the local stores.

An **Oatmeal Mask** is good for all skin types. Mix equal parts ground oatmeal and buttermilk in a bowl. Spread over face and neck. Relax and let dry. Rinse and it will leave your skin soft and moisturized.

A **Citrus Ginger Sugar Scrub** is also a great treatment idea. Mix together juice from a small lemon, ½ cup brown sugar, 2 tablespoons honey, and a teaspoon of grated ginger. Use it as an exfoliator for the face. Send it home as a party favor by putting the remainder in a small, old-fashioned mason jar. Wrap in burlap and tie with colored raffia.

Scented Lotions are also great spa party favors and are quick to make. Use plain unscented body lotion and try different essential oils to personalize your scent.

knit night

knitting circle

The word "knitting" usually conjures up images of little old ladies sitting quietly, working on a pair of baby booties or a shawl. Not so! Today's knitter is a vibrant young woman who enjoys creating fun, personalized accessories and gifts. Knitting is a great social project for many reasons. It doesn't take a lot of materials so it's easy to bring along. It's simple to do so you can carry on a conversation while working. It's relaxing and, if you keep your projects simple, instantly gratifying. One of the nicest things about knitting is that, even with imperfections, hand-knitted items have a personal charm that you just don't get from a store-bought knit. The fun part is personalizing your simple projects to make them uniquely YOU. Easy embellishments can turn a plain scarf or hat into a one-of-a-kind fashion statement. Just be careful not to get too attached to the things you intend to give as gifts. It can be so hard to let them go!

KNIT NIBBLES

Knitting tends to be more popular during chilly weather. So if you are creating cozy projects, you should serve comforting snacks as well. Bake up a batch of Classic Oat Cookies (see recipes page 59) for your guests to enjoy. If you don't have time to bake, stop into your local bakery and choose a dozen to take away. Serve the cookies in little batches ready to dunk into a steaming mug of Spiked Hot Chocolate (see recipes page 59). It's a good idea to mix up a batch of cocoa before the girls arrive and store it in a large thermos to keep it piping hot. Set out little dishes of marshmallows and chocolate sprinkles so the girls can help themselves.

planning your knit night

The best thing about knitting is that its list of materials is short. Wool and needles are the primary supplies. If you are an avid knitter, it's good to have a selection of needles in different sizes on hand. That way, you can share with the girls who are just starting out. Also, darning needles and scissors are useful for finishing off projects. Prior to your knit night, send out a list of wool shops in the area and specific styles to choose from.

Once you've chosen your knitting projects, you can start planning how you will embellish them to give them your own personal flair. This is the time to be creative and resourceful. Gather up all your left-over balls of wool as they can be used to create pompoms and tassels. Look around your house and you'll be surprised what you can find. Buttons are an easy way to add an accent to a simple scarf or hat. Fabric remnants are great to use to create patches and trims.

TIPS

- *It's easy to plan an event around a knit night. Turn an ordinary baby shower into a memorable evening by throwing a baby knits night. Either you can pick a cute baby gift to work on individually or everyone can contribute to a group gift. Each girl can knit a square and use them all to assemble a one-of-a-kind baby blanket.*

- *If you are tired of knitting the same old things for yourself, plan a knit-and-trade night. Once you're done with your project, trade it for another one made by a friend.*

- *The holiday season can be crazy and stressful. Organize a Christmas knit night and get a jump on your gift list while socializing with friends.*

*crafty
knits*

Chances are, if you are planning a knitting night, you and your girlfriends already know how to knit. It's helpful to have a few projects you can pass along that are easy to accomplish and fun to personalize. Here are some funky ideas that your guests can easily complete during your knit night.

BREEZY MOHAIR SHAWL

This is a terrific project because of its versatility. It is a fairly open knit, so the scarf can be worn more stretched out as a shawl or scrunched up around your neck as a scarf.

Start with one skein (approx. 440 yards) of 3 gauge mohair yarn. Using size 15 (10 mm) needles, cast on 40 stitches. Using a stocking knit stitch, knitting one row and then purling one row, repeat for approximately 2 yards. Cast off. You can find a variety of stylish ways to embellish this scarf. Weave slim ribbon in a matching color through the short edges of the scarf to create a girly trim. Tie small bows on all four corners. Sew a line of delicate buttons across the short edges of the scarf to give it a bit of sparkle.

SIMPLE CAP

This hat is another fast and fun knitting project that looks cute on every girl.

Start with one 100 gram hank (approximately 45 yards) of an Alpaca/Wool blend (Blue Sky Bulky hand-dyed is suggested). Using size 19 (15 mm) needles, cast on 29 stitches. Using stocking knit stitch (see above), knit until the project is about 6 inches (15 cm) from the beginning. To shape the top, begin reducing stitches by knitting a row as follows: knit one, *knit two together, knit two. After this, repeat from * to end of row leaving you with 22 stitches. Next row, purl one, *purl two together, purl two. After this, repeat from * to end of row leaving you with 15 stitches. Next row, knit one, *knit two together. Repeat from * to the end of row leaving you with 8 stitches. Last row, purl 2 together leaving 4 stitches. Cut yarn leaving about 12 inches (30 cm). Thread yarn through last four stitches and pull them together. Using the tail of the yarn, sew up seam and knot at bottom (brim).

movie madness

award-winning fun

Movie night has always been a mainstay for girls' night in. Just because it's not the newest of ideas doesn't mean you can't make an award-winning event out of it. With so many different types of movies to choose from, the theme possibilities are endless. Once you've picked your theme, let your imagination run riot! It's easy to think up ways to serve snacks, decor ideas, and intermission activities to create a spectacular effect.

A good old-fashioned pajama party is a great theme that lends itself to dozens of movies, old and new. Go crazy will all the fun and silliness of a teenage slumber party, complete with funny PJs and sleeping bags or do up a contemporary night in fantastic loungewear and gourmet snacks. Pick a classic horror movie to get the gang screaming or a modern chick flick oozing with romance and style. Invite a great group of girls, choose a fabulous film, and offer some cool movie snacks, and there definitely won't be any slumber at this party.

MOVIE MUNCHIES

There are certain must-have snacks for any movie night. The trick is to dress them up for your theme. A slumber party is a great excuse to go crazy with goodies. Instead of plain popcorn, spice it up with fresh Parmesan cheese and spices, or sweeten it with sugar and cinnamon. Serve in popcorn tubs covered in cute papers. Why have regular sodas and wine when you can whip up some "grown up" lemonade with a chilled Vodka Collins (see recipes page 60)? If you are aiming for a more low key night, old-fashioned lemonade is a must. Your guests will be giddy over Mini Burgers served with all the trimmings (see recipes page 60). And, of course, every respectable slumber party is loaded with candy. Choose candies and snacks that are all color-coordinated to your decor. Have tubs of candies and treats scattered throughout the room for easy access or lay it all out as a buffet for the girls to graze on throughout the movie.

private screening

Planning a pajama party is as easy as it was back in the day. Add a few grown-up treats to the basic idea and you've got it. Clear away the furniture and roll out the sleeping bags (or tell the girls to bring their own). Toss soft throw blankets around the room and light lots of candles for a cozy atmosphere. Bring out loads of bed pillows with fun, colorful linens. If a pillow fight ensues, you'll know you're not as grown up as you think you are!

Use your most vibrant table linens and dishes and decorate a table with balloons and movie tickets. Ask your girlfriends to wear their silliest PJs and craziest socks. You might want to provide fuzzy slippers for your guests as a laugh. If you're sending out invites, create a one-of-a kind "Girls Only" membership card. Make sure to specify that there are most certainly NO BOYS ALLOWED!

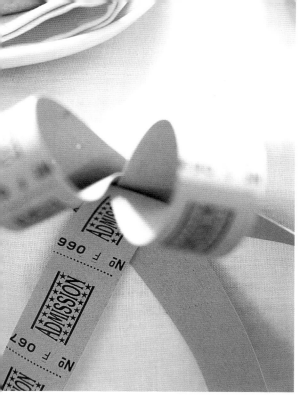

TIPS

- *Can't think of a movie theme? Take it from the movie title itself. The Pink Panther, "pretty in pink," "pink flamingos".... see where this is going?*

- *Don't want to spend the evening indoors? Grab an extension cord, move the TV outside, and make it movies alfresco. Lay a big blanket on the lawn or tell the girls to bring their beach chairs.*

- *Stop the movie in the middle and have an intermission. Make it a snack break, recap what's happened so far, or just stretch your legs.*

- *Make it an award-winning night and have ballots for your guests to fill out. They can be categories such as "best dressed," "best movie star attitude," or "best movie commentary". Give a silly award at the end of the evening like a Barbie doll spray-painted gold.*

chick flicks & fright nights

When you pick your movie theme, think about every aspect of the night that can tie into it. When sending invitations, include a questionnaire asking what everyone's favorite movie is. This will help narrow down your choices. Keep the decor colorful and fun. Think about what ties into your theme. You can keep it as simple as choosing food and drinks that complement your theme or you can go all out and dress up your house and your guests in everything that your theme suggests.

All-American Bust out all your leftover Fourth of July paper plates and napkins, or anything red, white, and blue. Serve popcorn in old-fashioned paper buckets.

Bella Italia Make your guests an offer they can't refuse. *Godfather*, spaghetti westerns, and spaghetti dinner.

Chick Flicks When you wanna laugh, cry, or just be girls together. Throw in some movie theater-style candy and feel the girl power.

Retro 1970s or 1980s Pick a decade and choose the movies that made them famous. Ask your guests to dress for the era. Maybe hold a disco or 1980s dance-off at intermission?

Bollywood Blowout Serve samosas and tandoori while while enjoying some of India's finest cinematic exports. Throw colorful sari material over furniture and transform your living room into an Eastern paradise.

Fright Fest Bloody movies and Bloody Marys? Scream and ice cream? Mix up scary snacks and a cocktail to die for and the girls will be shrieking with delight.

Kung Fu Fever Order in some Chinese food, turn off the volume, and make up your own dialogue.

valentines & cocktails

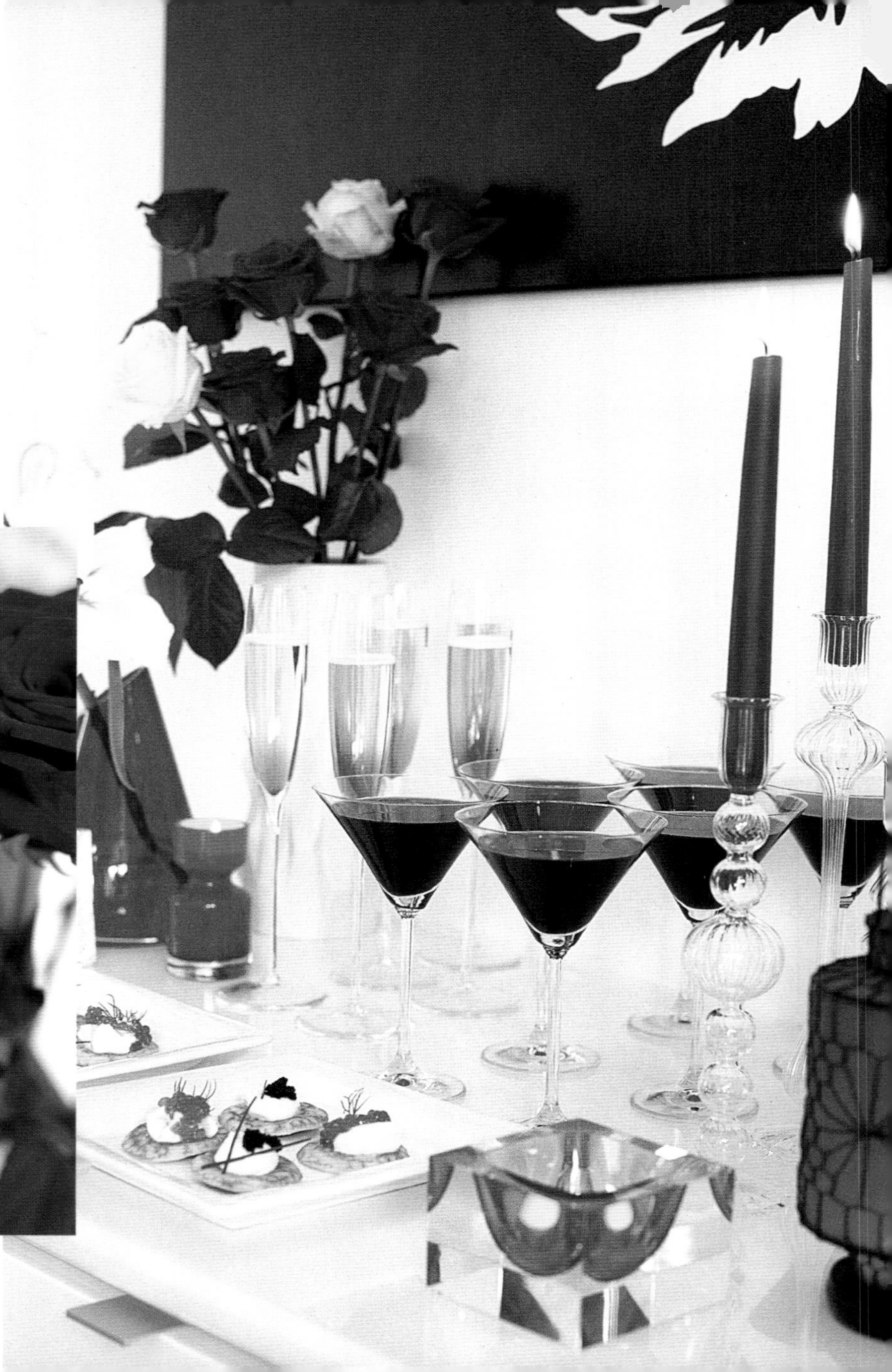

lovefest

Valentine's Day generally has two meanings for the modern woman, depending upon her current romantic situation. There's the happy couple version: a woman in love sees Valentine's Day as the ultimate romantic occasion, a day filled with flowers, chocolates, and *amore*. The single girl sees Valentine's Day as a celebration of sisterhood, replacing the traditional ideas of romance with a fun salute to their girlfriends. A true Girls' Night In will embrace both of these takes on Valentine's Day. Gather all the girls together and put their creative sides to work with fun valentine card projects. Indulge your friends with sinful snacks and sexy cocktails. Whether they are creating the most romantic and heartfelt valentine for their loved one, or competing to see who can make the most over-the-top greeting card for a friend, this night is all about love.

TREATS FOR YOUR SWEETS

Sweet indulgences are a symbol of Valentine's Day. Why not put a contemporary spin on some holiday favorites? Instead of classic champagne or martinis, mix up pitchers of sweet and fruity

Cherry Martinis or Kir Royales (see recipes page 61). Be sure and serve them in your most fabulous and sleek glassware. Serve up small and delicate snacks and garnish them to look classy and decadent. Top Cocktail Blini with smoked salmon and crème fraîche (sour cream works, too). Garnish with a sprig of fresh dill, serve on your fanciest platter, and your guests will think you hired a caterer. Create a deliciously sweet dessert fondue station by serving bowls of fresh fruit, small cookies, brownies, and cakes along with melted chocolate in a fondue pot. Since most girls can never have too much chocolate, go all out and get the biggest box of the best chocs you can find. It's guaranteed not to go to waste!

Indulge your friends with sinful snacks and sexy cocktails.

A night of valentines and cocktails is simple to prepare for. Chances are, you have most of the supplies around your house already. Set the date of your night to land a week or so before Valentine's Day so that the cards that need to be mailed will reach their destination on time. Also, it won't interfere with any romantic plans some of the girls may already have. Create a fun, feminine mood by decorating with small vases of pink or red roses and small candles scattered about the house. Sprinkle conversation hearts on tables. They are a great addition to any valentines card and are an adorable addition to the decor. Cover tables with craft paper so girls can feel free to create their valentine masterpieces without fear of making a mess. Place card-making supplies in the middle of the table so everyone can share. Set up your refreshments as a buffet nearby so girls can take breaks from their art to enjoy a cocktail and a snack.

make a date

Create a fun, feminine mood by decorating with small vases of pink or red roses and small candles scattered about the house.

TIPS

- *Ask the girls to bring along some good love song CDs to get you in the mood.*

- *For a truly festive atmosphere, tell your friends to dress in their girliest pinks and reds. Snap pictures of the girls with a Polaroid or digital camera and use the photos as part of the Valentine's Day cards.*

- *Have a few books of poetry around to lend some romantic words to a beautiful card.*

- *If cost is an issue, invite the girls to bring along their favorite sweet treats and turn the evening into a sweets swap. This way, you can all taste something new and delicious and everyone goes home with a tasty party favor.*

- *If Valentines don't suit you and your gang, change up the crafts and turn your event into a Christmas card factory. This will combine your holiday tasks with a great seasonal get-together.*

be mine...

The great thing about constructing homemade valentines cards is that anything goes! You can be as traditional or as crazy as you like and the recipient will love it. Here is a list of some different materials to make cards. Look around and you'll certainly find more than you need to create museum-worthy cards.

MATERIALS

Construction paper	Postcards
Fabric remnants	Craft glue
Buttons	Scissors
Glitter	Stapler
Ribbons	Darning needles
Doilies	Embroidery threads
Small pompoms	Hole punchers
Silk flowers and leaves	Cookie cutters
Magazines	

ONE-OF-A-KIND GREETINGS

Valentine fortunes Cut 4-inch (10 cm) circles out of construction paper. Fold in the middle and then bring points together. Staple the edges underneath. You now have a paper fortune "cookie." Slide romantic notes and fortunes inside such as "You will kiss a handsome stranger" or "Someone has a crush on you." Deliver them in a small paper Chinese food container.

Bee mine flowerpot Cut out a large rectangle with colored construction paper. Then cut out the shape of a flowerpot in a different color and staple onto the rectangle, leaving the top of the pot open. Take silk leaves with wire stems and glue flower shapes on to them so that it becomes a flower stem. Slide stems into flowerpot and arrange. Draw a bee, buzzing on the flowerpot, with the words "Bee mine."

Ransom note card Cut out letters from magazines and assemble an anonymous "Ransom note." You can say things like "You're holding my heart hostage" or arrange a clandestine meeting to surprise a secret crush.

recipes

ROASTED NUTS

The number one rule—fresh nuts and freshly ground spices.

freshly ground or crushed spices such as cardamom, nutmeg, cumin seeds, paprika

fresh raw nuts (about 1 oz. or 2 tablespoons per person) such as peanuts, cashews, macadamias, almonds, pecans

1 tablespoon sunflower oil, for roasting (optional)

sea salt flakes

Serves 8

To roast the nuts, heat a dry skillet, add one kind of nut and cook, shaking the pan, until they're aromatic and slightly golden. You must stay with them and keep shaking, or the nuts will burn and be spoiled. When ready, tip them into a wide, shallow bowl, then sprinkle with salt and one of the spices. To serve, put about 4 tablespoons of the nuts into a tiny china bowl or silver dish and serve.

CHEESE STRAWS

Home-made cheese straws taste better than the bought variety, and are very easy to make.

1 cup all-purpose flour

½ teaspoon sea salt

1 teaspoon dry mustard powder

½ cup grated Cheddar cheese

2 tablespoons freshly grated Parmesan cheese

5 tablespoons butter, chilled and diced

1 egg yolk

juice of ½ lemon

several baking trays, greased

Makes 36

Put the flour, salt, mustard, and both cheeses in a food processor and pulse to mix. Add the butter and pulse until the mixture resembles fine crumbs.

Mix the egg yolk and lemon juice in a small pitcher, then pour into the processor with the motor running. Stop mixing when the mixture forms a ball, then transfer to a floured surface and knead briefly to form a ball.

Roll out to a rectangle about ⅛ inch thick. Using a hot, sharp knife, cut into strips 3 x ½ inch. Twist into spirals and arrange apart on baking trays.

Bake in a preheated oven at 350°F for 10 minutes until golden. Remove from the oven, dust with paprika if using, then cool on the baking tray. Serve in small glasses.

COSMOPOLITAN

The TV show Sex and the City made this drink popular: its great taste has ensured it stays that way.

2 oz. lemon vodka

1 oz. triple sec

1 oz. lime juice

1 oz. cranberry juice

Add all the ingredients to a shaker filled with ice, shake sharply and strain into a frosted martini glass.

MINI SPRING ROLLS

Make these in advance, then reheat in the oven before serving.

1 oz. beanthread (cellophane) noodles (1 small bundle)

5 Chinese dried cloud ear mushrooms, finely diced

8 oz. ground pork

½ onion, finely chopped

3 garlic cloves, crushed

3 scallions, finely sliced

¼ cup crabmeat

sea salt and freshly ground black pepper

1 package large Vietnamese ricepaper wrappers (50 sheets)

peanut or safflower oil, for frying

Makes about 40 mini rolls

Soak the noodles in hot water for 20 minutes. Drain and snip into short lengths. Soak the dried mushrooms in boiling water to cover for 30 minutes, then drain and chop. Put the noodles, mushrooms, pork, onion, garlic, scallions, crabmeat, salt, and pepper in a food processor and pulse to mix.

Put 4 ricepapers in a bowl of warm water and let soften for 1–2 minutes. Cut each one into 4 segments. Put 1 segment on a work surface, put 1 teaspoon of filling next to the curved edge, and pat the filling into a small cylinder. Fold the curved edge over the filling, fold over the 2 sides like an envelope, then roll up towards the long pointed end. Press to seal. Repeat with all the other wrappers.

Fill a wok one-third full of peanut oil and heat to 375°F or until a piece of noodle fluffs up immediately. Put 5–6 spring rolls in the oil and fry until crisp and golden. Remove and drain on paper towels. Repeat until all the spring rolls are cooked. Serve.

SHRIMP WITH CHILE MOJO

An easy recipe with one simple requirement—perfect shrimp.

3 cooked shrimp per person

¼ cup chopped fresh flat-leaf parsley

1 tablespoon chopped oregano or marjoram

a pinch of salt and a pinch of sugar

3 garlic cloves, minced

grated zest of 1 lime

½ cup freshly squeezed lime juice

1 large red chile, cored, seeded, and finely chopped

Makes about 1 cup

Put the herbs, salt, sugar, garlic, lime zest, and lime juice in a blender and work until smooth. Transfer to a serving dish and stir in the chopped chile.

Put the fresh shrimp on a plate with a bowl of Chile Mojo and serve.

GIBSON MARTINI

This classic drink has truly withstood the test of time.

a dash of vermouth

1½ oz. well-chilled gin or vodka

silverskin onion, to garnish

Makes 1

Add the ingredients to a mixing glass filled with ice and stir. Strain into a martini glass and garnish.

HUMMUS WITH FLAT BEANS

This irresistible combination will leave your friends wanting more.

1 lb. flat beans or runner beans

1 cup hummus, either store-bought or homemade

To serve
2 teaspoons extra-virgin olive oil

freshly cracked black pepper

Serves 6–8

Top and tail the beans, then cut them diagonally into 1–2-inch sections.

Spoon the hummus into a small bowl and swirl the top. Sprinkle with olive oil and pepper, if using. Put the bowl on a serving platter with the beans beside.

SUSHI

For a party, prepare at least 3 kinds, with one of each kind per person.

The rice
2 cups sushi rice

Sushi vinegar

⅔ cup Japanese rice vinegar

⅓ cup sugar

4 teaspoons sea salt

3 inches fresh ginger, grated, then squeezed in a garlic crusher

3 garlic cloves, crushed

Makes 2 sushi rolls, 6 slices each

Wash the rice 5 times in cold water. Let drain in a strainer for at least 30 minutes, or overnight.

Put in a saucepan with 2⅓ cups water (the same volume of water plus 15 percent more). Cover tightly and bring to a boil over high heat. Reduce the heat to medium and boil for 10 minutes. Reduce to low and simmer for 5 minutes.

Do not raise the lid. Still covered, let rest for 10 minutes.

Put the vinegar, sugar, salt, ginger, and garlic in a saucepan and heat gently.

Spread the rice over a wide dish, cut through with a rice paddle or wooden spoon, and fan to cool. Cut the vinegar mixture through the rice with the spoon.

Use immediately while still tepid. Do not chill—cold spoils sushi. (The rice contains vinegar, which will preserve it for a short time.)

The rice is now ready to be assembled in the recipe, below.

The sushi
1 sheet nori seaweed, toasted

1 quantity sushi rice (left)

½ teaspoon wasabi paste

1 mini cucumber, 1 slice smoked salmon, 1 avocado

To serve
Japanese tamari soy sauce (which is made without wheat)

pink pickled ginger

wasabi paste

Makes 12

Cut the seaweed in half. Put one piece on a bamboo sushi mat, shiny side down. Divide the rice in half and press each portion into a cylinder shape. Put one cylinder in the middle of one piece of seaweed and press out the rice to meet the front edge. Press toward the far edge, leaving about ½–1 inch bare.

Brush ¼ teaspoon wasabi down the middle of the rice and put a line of cucumber (or filling of your choice) on top.

Roll the mat gently from the front edge, pinch gently, then complete the roll and squeeze to make a tight cylinder. Make a second cylinder using the remaining ingredients.

The sushi can be wrapped in plastic and left like this until you are ready to cut and serve. To serve, cut in half with a wet knife and trim off the end. Cut each half in 3 and arrange on a serving platter.

MOJITO
A refreshing cocktail—ideal for a relaxing evening with friends.

5 mint sprigs

2 oz. golden rum

a dash of fresh lime juice

2 dashes of simple syrup

soda water, to top up

Makes 1

Put the mint in a highball glass, add the rum, lime juice, and simple syrup and muddle with a barspoon until the aroma of the mint is released. Add crushed ice and stir until the mixture and the mint is spread evenly. Top with soda water and stir again. Serve with straws.

CLASSIC OAT COOKIES
Delicious whether plain or flavored with dried fruit.

1 stick unsalted butter, very soft

¾ cup light brown sugar

1 large egg, beaten

1 tablespoon milk

½ teaspoon vanilla essence

¾ cup self-rising flour

½ cup dried fruit (raisins, cherries, cranberries, or blueberries)

1 ½ cups porridge oats

several baking sheets, lightly greased

Makes 24

Put the butter, sugar, egg, milk, and vanilla in a bowl and beat well using an electric mixer or whisk, or a wooden spoon. Add the flour, dried fruit, and oats and mix well with the wooden spoon.

Put heaped teaspoons of dough onto the prepared baking sheets, spacing them well apart. Bake in a preheated oven at 350°F Gas 4 for 12–15 minutes until lightly browned around the edges. Let cool on the sheets for 2 minutes, then transfer to a wire rack to cool completely.

SPIKED HOT CHOCOLATE
A warming drink with a kick.

32 ounces milk

1 cup cocoa

½ cup Cointreau

Makes 8

Heat milk and cocoa in a medium saucepan until steaming, stirring frequently. Pour into large ceramic pitcher or thermos. Add Cointreau.

MINI BURGERS

These mini morsels look good and taste great.

40 mini hamburger buns

barbecue sauce or chilli sauce

baby salad and herb leaves

10 cherry tomatoes, sliced

4 baby onions, finely sliced

40 baby cornichons (gherkins)

Hamburger patties
2 cups finely ground lean beef

4 small onions, finely chopped

3 garlic cloves, crushed

1 red chilli, deseeded and finely chopped

1 egg, beaten

a pinch of freshly ground nutmeg

¼ cup fresh white breadcrumbs

salt and freshly grated black pepper

peanut oil, for frying

Makes 40

Put all the patty ingredients except the oil in a bowl and mix well. Take 1 tablespoon of the mixture and shape into a round, flat patty. Repeat until all the mixture is used. Heat a film of oil in a heavy-based frying pan until very hot, then add a layer of patties, spaced well apart. Fry for 2–3 minutes, turning half way, until cooked through. Remove from the pan, drain on crumpled kitchen paper and keep them warm while you cook the remaining patties.

Split the buns, leaving one side attached if possible. Put a dot of barbecue sauce or chilli sauce into each bun, then a salad leaf, a patty, tomato and onion ring. Put the lid on the bun and secure with a cocktail stick and a mini cornichon.

POPCORN

Popcorn can be made up to a day ahead, but store it in an airtight container so it stays crisp.

3 tablespoons vegetable oil

4 oz. popcorn kernels

6 tablespoons honey (or flavouring of your choice)

4 tablespoons butter

Makes about 4 tubs

Heat 1 tablespoon oil in a large, heavy-bottomed pan over a high heat. Add a third of the corn kernels, cover, and cook, shaking the pan constantly, until all the kernels have popped.
 Remove from the heat and transfer the popcorn to a large bowl. Add the honey and the butter to the empty saucepan and melt together. Return the popcorn to the pan and toss through the butter, then set aside.

VODKA COLLINS

Try the Vodka Collins for a sharp, zingy, thirst quencher.

2 oz. Vox vodka

¾ oz. fresh lemon juice

½ oz. simple syrup

club soda, to top up

lemon slice, to garnish

Build the ingredients into a highball glass filled with ice. Stir gently and garnish with a lemon slice. Serve with two straws.

COCKTAIL BLINI

You can buy cocktail blini in many delicatessens, but usually they're not made authentically with buckwheat flour.

1 cup buckwheat flour or half-and-half with all-purpose flour

1 package (¼ oz.) active dried yeast

1 teaspoon sea salt

1 egg, separated

1 teaspoon sugar

¾ cup lukewarm milk

1 tablespoon butter, for sautéing

To serve
crème fraîche or sour cream

caviar and/or salmon keta

herbs, such as snipped chives and dill sprigs

about 4 pieces smoked salmon, finely sliced

Makes 24

Mix the flour, yeast, and salt in a bowl and make a hollow in the center. Beat the egg yolk with the sugar and ¾ cup warm water and add to the hollow. Mix well, then cover with a damp cloth and let rise at room temperature until doubled in size, about 2 hours.

Beat in the milk to make a thick, creamy batter. Cover again and leave for 1 hour until small bubbles appear on the surface.

Beat the egg white to soft peak stage, then fold it into the batter.

Heat a heavy skillet or crêpe pan and brush with butter. Drop in about 1 teaspoon of batter to make a pancake about 1 inch in diameter. Cook until the surface bubbles, about 2–3 minutes, then flip it over with a spatula and cook the second side for 2 minutes.

Put on a plate in the oven to keep warm while you cook the remaining blini. Don't put the blini on top of each other. Serve warm.

To serve, top with a spoonful of crème fraîche or sour cream, snipped chives or dill sprigs, and a small pile of caviar or keta or a curl of smoked salmon.

CHERRY MARTINI

This martini can also be made using the juice from canned cherries—it may not sound nice on paper but wait until you taste it!

3 stoned fresh cherries

2 oz. vodka

2 oz. thick cherry juice

a dash of cherry schnapps

Crush the cherries in a shaker using the flat end of a barspoon. Add ice and the remaining ingredients, shake sharply and strain through a sieve into a frosted martini glass.

KIR ROYALE

After a shaky start, the Kir Royale is now the epitome of chic sophistication.

a dash of crème de cassis

champagne, to top up

Add a small dash of crème de cassis to a champagne flute and gently top with champagne. Stir gently and serve.

STOCKISTS

Fashion & Accessories

BRORA
81 Marylebone High Street
London W1U 4QJ, UK
+44 (0)20 7224 5040
+44 (0)20 7736 9944
for mail order
www.brora.com
Classic cashmere, woollen
and tweed clothing for men,
women, and children.

EMMA CASSI
48a White Hart Lane
London SW13 OPZ, UK
+44 (0)7092 193 316
www.emmacassi.com
Creates beautiful accessories
using vintage lace, hand
embroidered with buttons,
sequins, and glass beads.

HARRISON-LONDON
The Studio
33 Malvern Road
London E8 3LP, UK
+44 (0)20 7683 0577
www.harrison-london.co.uk
Dresses and separates in
luxurious fabrics
characterized by quirky
cuts, layering, and exquisite
details.

IRIS
73 Salusbury Road
London NW6 6NJ, UK
+44 (0)20 7372 1777
info@irisfashion.co.uk
The quintessential feminine
boutique selling hot new
fashion labels, stylish
maternity wear, beautiful
underwear, and adorable
children's clothes.

MARCCO + TRUMP
146 Columbia Road
London E2 7RG, UK
+44 (0)7956 465 126
Vintage cocktail dresses and
shoes from the 1940s and
1950s, vintage jewelry,
original cocktail shakers,
glasses, and crockery.

MAX OLIVER
100 Islington High Street
Camden Passage
London N1 8EG, UK
+44 (0)20 7354 0777
www.max-oliver.co.uk
Luxury lifestyle boutique
specializing in chandeliers
and decorative antiques,
French and vintage style
clothing and textiles, gifts,
jewelry, accessories, and
homeware.

RED OR DEAD
www.redordead.com
+44 (0)20 7288 9853
Unique, daring, and
accessible British design
brand with a fresh attitude,
selling shoes and fashion.

Furniture & Home Accessories

BED BATH AND BEYOND
800 462 3966
www.bedbathandbeyond.com
Home and bath decor,
tableware, and linens.

CATH KIDSTON
8 Clarendon Cross
London W11, UK
+44 (0)20 7221 4248 for
stores and stockists
+44 (0)20 7221 8000 for
mail order
www.cathkidston.co.uk
1950s inspired floral print
fabrics; cushions, pajamas,
slippers, and homeware.

CLIO
92 Thompson Street
New York, NY 10013
212 966 8991
www.clio-home.com
Tableware, linens,
home decor.

COUVERTURE
310 King's Road
Chelsea
London SW3 5UH, UK
+44 (0)20 7795 1200
info@couverture.co.uk
www.couverture.co.uk
Retro-style knitted cushions,
throws, embroidered
bedlinen and nightwear,
children's toys, and
homeware—all with an
exquisite hand-crafted feel.

THE CONRAN SHOP
81 Fulham Road
London SW3 6RD, UK
+44 (0)20 7589 7401 for
stores and stockists
www.conran.com
The Conran Shop represents
a vast selection of different
types of homeware products,
traditional as well as
contemporary.

CRATE AND BARREL
800 967 6696
www.crateandbarrel.com
Tableware, linens, home
decor.

DYPTIQUE
195 Westbourne Grove
London W11 2BB. UK
+44 (0)20 7727 8673 for
stores and stockists
www.dyptiqueparis.com
World-famous range of
scented candles and soaps.

GRAHAM & GREEN
4 & 10 Elgin Crescent
London W11 2HX. UK
+44 (0)845 130 6622 for
mail order
www.grahamandgreen.co.uk
Glamorous products for you
and your home, including
mirrored furniture, lighting,
bedlinen, and nightwear.

HABITAT
196 Tottenham Court Road
London W1T 7LG. UK
+44 (0)845 601 0740
www.habitat.net
Everything for the modern
home, including furniture,
glassware, kitchenware, soft
furnishings, and lighting.

HOUSE OF FRASER
318 Oxford Street
London W1C 1HF. UK
+44 (0)20 7529 4700
+44 (0)870 963 2591
for stockists

www.houseoffraser.co.uk
The Linea Home Furniture
collection includes furniture
and home accessories for
bed, bath, and dining.

MAISONETTE
79 Chamberlayne Road
London NW10 3ND. UK
+44 (0)20 8964 8444
maisonetteUK@aol.com
www.maisonette.uk.com
1970s and retro style
glassware, lamps, vintage
silk cushions, and luxury
items for the home.

OBJET TROUVE
23a Ezra Street
Columbia Road
London E2 7RH. UK
Beautiful and ornamental
French antique furniture.
+44 (0)7779 265 554

PEARL RIVER MART
477 Broadway
New York, NY 10013
800 878 2446
www.pearlriver.com
Home and bath decor,
tableware, paper products.

VOODOO BLUE
6a Victoria Parade
Sandycoombe Road
Kew
Richmond TW9 3NB. UK
+44 (0)20 8560 7050 for
stockists and mail order
www.voodooblue.co.uk
Fair-trade hand-woven sisal
baskets from Kenya in a
wide range of colors and sizes.

THE WHITE COMPANY
12 Marylebone High Street
London W1U 4NR. UK
+44 (0)870 900 7879 for
stores, stockists, and mail order
www.thewhitecompany.com
Luxury bedlinen, bedding,
soft furnishings, and quality
home accessories.

Miscellaneous

THE BEAD SHOP
21a Tower Street
Covent Garden
London WC2H 2NS. UK
+44 (0)20 7240 0931
www.beadworks.co.uk
A huge range of beads and
all that you would require to
make your own jewelry.

KATE'S PAPERIE
800 809 9880
www.katespaperie.com
Invitations and paper
products.

PURL
137 Sullivan Street
New York, NY 10012
800 597 PURL
www.purlsoho.com
Yarn and knitting materials.

PAPERCHASE
12 Alfred Place
London WC1E 7EB. UK
+44 (0)20 7467 6200 for
stockists and enquiries
www.paperchase.co.uk
Design led and innovative
stationery.

TINSEL TRADING CO.
47 West 28th Street
New York, NY 10018
www.tinseltrading.com
Vintage flowers, trims,
and notions.

CONVERSION CHARTS

Weights and measures have been rounded up or down slightly to make measuring easier.

VOLUME EQUIVALENTS

american	metric	imperial
1 teaspoon	5 ml	
1 tablespoon	15 ml	
1/4 cup	60 ml	2 fl.oz.
1/3 cup	75 ml	2 1/2 fl.oz.
1/2 cup	125 ml	4 fl.oz.
2/3 cup	150 ml	5 fl.oz. (1/4 pint)
3/4 cup	175 ml	6 fl.oz.
1 cup	250 ml	8 fl.oz.

WEIGHT EQUIVALENTS:

imperial	metric
1 oz.	25 g
2 oz.	50 g
3 oz.	75 g
4 oz.	125 g
5 oz.	150 g
6 oz.	175 g
7 oz.	200 g
8 oz. (1/2 lb.)	250 g
9 oz.	275 g
10 oz.	300 g
11 oz.	325 g
12 oz.	375 g
13 oz.	400 g
14 oz.	425 g
15 oz.	475 g
16 oz. (1 lb.)	500 g
2 1b.	1 kg

MEASUREMENTS:

inches	cm
1/4 inch	5 mm
1/2 inch	1 cm
3/4 inch	1.5 cm
1 inch	2.5 cm
2 inches	5 cm
3 inches	7 cm
4 inches	10 cm
5 inches	12 cm
6 inches	15 cm
7 inches	18 cm
8 inches	20 cm
9 inches	23 cm
10 inches	25 cm
11 inches	28 cm
12 inches	30 cm

OVEN TEMPERATURES:

225°F	110°C	Gas 1/4
250°F	120°C	Gas 1/2
275°F	140°C	Gas 1
300°F	150°C	Gas 2
325°F	160°C	Gas 3
350°F	180°C	Gas 4
375°F	190°C	Gas 5
400°F	200°C	Gas 6
425°F	220°C	Gas 7
450°F	230°C	Gas 8
475°F	240°C	Gas 9

THE PUBLISHER WOULD LIKE TO THANK THE FOLLOWING:

Nicky Crancher
Hair Stylist
+++ (0)1708 781729

Elkie Brown
Stylist (in training)
elkiebrown@hotmail.com

Sam Neat and Collette McGee
Hair Stylists
Represented by
Windle Hair Salon
41–45 Shorts Gardens
London WC2H 9AP, UK
+++ (0)20 7497 2393

Thank you to all our lovely models, especially Kate, Gemma, Raquel, Jessica, Louise, Kirsten, Stephanie, Emily, Alicia, Christina, Natalie, Emily, Kat, Alis, Louisa, Tamra, Lucille, Becca, Dee, Michelle, Georgina, Becky, Shan, and Holly.

Very special thanks to Vicki Casselson at Eyecandy Model and Promotions Agency www.eyecandy-promo.co.uk and Alex J at CAPE London Limited www.capelondon.com.

Recipes
ELSA PETERSEN-SCHEPELERN
Roasted Nuts
Cheese Straws
Mini Spring Rolls
Shrimp with Chile Mojo
Hummus with Flat Beans
Sushi
Mini Burgers
Cocktail Blini

LINDA COLLISTER
Oat Cookies

BEN REED
Cosmopolitan
Gibson Martini
Mojito
Vodka Collins
Kir Royale
Cherry Martini

I would like to thank Lena Tabori and Colleen Mullaney for their invaluable advice and guidance. Thank you to Shelton and Penny for opening up your homes for "practice" Girls' Nights, as well as Sonya, Laura, Missi, Allison, Nancy, Jill, and Kristen for making them as fun as the real thing. Thanks to Claire Richardson for taking such lovely photographs. I would also like to thank Miriam Hyslop, Alison Starling, and everyone at RPS.

I would especially like to thank my Mom, Gayle, for all of her love and support and for teaching me how to be great hostess. I learned from the best.

acknowledgements